Printed in Spain

This 1989 edition published by Derrydale Books,
distributed by Crown Publishers, Inc., 225 Park Avenue
South, New York, New York 10003.

ISBN: 0-517-64954-3

The City Mouse

and the

Country Mouse

Illustrated by Graham Percy

DERRYDALE BOOKS
New York

O nce upon a time there was a happy country mouse who had a vistor. His visitor was an old friend who came from the court of the King.

The country mouse fetched
all his best cheeses and
bacon for his guest.

Then he served young, tender corn and freshly
baked bread.

And from the spring in the forest nearby, he
brought the purest sparkling water for them to drink.

After this wonderful meal the two mice sat beside the fire and chatted.

"I cannot understand," said the town mouse, "how you can bear to live in this gloomy place and put up with this dull country food!"

"Why, at court there's no end of fine feasting and,
what's more, there is lots of dancing and all kinds of
merriment.
But you must see it all for yourself!
Come with me when I return there tomorrow."

"I'll think about," said the country mouse "and I'll tell you what I decide in the morning."

Early the next morning the country mouse greeted his friend. "Good morning," he said, "I've made up my mind. Yes, I'd like to come along with you!"

All day the two friends walked and
walked and when at last they reached
the royal court it was very late.

But in the great banquet hall there were the remains of an elegant feast.

So the two mice enjoyed all sorts of puddings and sweets...

and they even shared a little champagne.

But just as they were about to start eating some fine, rare cheeses they suddenly heard the barking and scratching of a big dog.

And then, they were even more frightened when they
heard a cat meow!

Then they heard the tramp, tramp of the servants as they came to clear away the tables.

All of the noise sent the city mouse off to his hole so quickly that he didn't have time to show the way to the poor little country mouse

who was very frightened and had only the tassle of a curtain to hide behind.

When all was quiet again, the city mouse came out to look for his friend. When he found him, the two quickly ran back to the city mouse's elegant rooms behind the walls of the banquet hall.

There the country mouse said quietly but very firmly, "If all this fine eating and wonderful living is always interrupted by such awful alarms and dangers, then I prefer to go back to my plain food and my simple cottage and the peace and quiet of the countryside."

"But won't you stay here for the night?" asked the city mouse.

24

"No thank you, I've had quite enough of your life in the great court," the country mouse called back as he scuttled down the ivy into the palace yard.

Then he darted quietly past the big shiny boots of
the guards

and out under the great iron gates and into the
night.

And he didn't stop running until he reached his own little cottage. The sun was coming up and all was quiet.

The country mouse was very happy to be home again.